A Horse,

Of Course!

By Kacy Carlson

Illustrated by Tanya Leontyeva

What can dance on

a log with a frog?

A horse, of course!

What can swing with

me from a tree?

A horse, of course!

What can sleep with

its head out of bed?

A horse, of course!

What can stand a

cat on a bat?

A horse, of course!

What can sit in some

chairs on the stairs?

A horse, of course!

What can run with a cane

through the rain?

A horse, of course!

What can jump with a

rose on its nose?

A horse, of course!

What can eat a bite

from a kite?

A horse, of course!

What can drink from a

jar in a car?

A horse, of course!

What can play in the barn

with some yarn?

A horse, of course!

What can climb up

a pole in a hole?

A horse, of course!

What can fight a fire

with a tire?

A horse, of course!

What can play with

a bug on a rug?

A horse, of course!

What can spin and

kick a stick?

A horse, of course!

What can drive with

a duck in a truck?

A horse, of course!

What can hug

my mother

and brother?

My horse, of course,

And me!

Made in the USA
Monee, IL
11 September 2020

41981064R00024